PRINCE ADITH LEARNS TO SHARE

Es Noonan and Muslima Keya

Dedicated to

The loves of my life
(they know who they are)

Hi. My name is Adith, but my parents call me Prince Adith because they say I behave like a royal prince born in a palace.

I don't know about that...AnywayI like going to Nursery and playing with my friends.

Sometimes, I get into trouble with my teacher, Mrs. Jones, because I don't like to share toys with my friends. Today is one of those days...here's my story.

Prince Adith, a curious little boy, recently started attending nursery.

He loves the new environment but has one issue, SHARING. Mrs. Jones, his teacher, notices Adith's trouble with sharing and decides to teach him the importance of sharing.

The next day, Mrs. Jones plans a storytelling session.

She started telling a story about sharing, hoping Adith would learn.

The story was about a little rabbit who learned to share its food with others.

Adith was captivated by the story.

After the storytelling session, the children were allowed to play.

Adith quickly grabbed his favorite truck but didn't let anyone else touch it.

Mrs. Jones notices this and reminds Adith of the story they had just heard.

She explained how sharing can bring happiness.

The next day, during art time, Adith has most of the bright crayons. Some of his classmates don't have many colors.

Adith is sitting around a table with other children, they are drawing pictures, and Adith has six crayons.

Remembering the story and Mrs. Jones' words, Adith decides to share his crayons.

His classmates were so happy to use bright colours on their pictures.

The following day, during a school picnic, in his lunch bag, Adith has packed his favorite chocolates, among his lunch.

He sees his friends looking at them and remembers the story of 'The Kind Rabbit'.

Adith decides to share his chocolates with his friends.

They all enjoyed the treat, and Adith felt delighted to see his friends happy.

Over the next few days, Adith became very good at sharing toys, crayons, or snacks, He was always ready to share.

Seeing the positive change in Adith,
Mrs. Jones was proud.

She praised Adith and told his story
to other children, encouraging them
to share as well.

Adith continues to share and becomes popular among his classmates. His acts of kindness encouraged other kids to share as well.

Mrs. Jones was pleased to see the positive change in her class.
She realized the power of storytelling and planned to use it more often to teach children the joy of sharing and being kind.